Ten Pink Piglets

GARTH PIG'S WALL SONG

by MARY RAYNER

Dutton Children's Books · New York

CIP Data is available.

First published in the United States 1994 by Dutton Children's Books,
a division of Penguin Books USA Inc., 375 Hudson Street, New York, New York 10014.
Originally published in Great Britain 1994 by Macmillan Children's Books, London.
Typography by Adrian Leichter
Printed in Singapore   First American Edition
1 3 5 7 9 10 8 6 4 2
ISBN 0-525-45241-9

Ten pink piglets up on the wall,

Ten pink piglets,

If one of those piglets should happen to fall,
Nine pink piglets up on the wall.

Nine pink piglets up on the wall,
Nine pink piglets,

If one of those piglets should happen to fall,
Eight pink piglets up on the wall.

Eight pink piglets up on the wall,
Eight pink piglets,

If one of those piglets should happen to fall,
Seven pink piglets up on the wall.

Seven pink piglets up on the wall,
Seven pink piglets,

If one of those piglets should happen to fall,
Six pink piglets up on the wall.

Six pink piglets up on the wall,
Six pink piglets,

If one of those piglets should happen to fall,
Five pink piglets up on the wall.

Five pink piglets up on the wall,
Five pink piglets,

If one of those piglets should happen to fall,
Four pink piglets up on the wall.

Four pink piglets up on the wall,
Four pink piglets,

If one of those piglets should happen to fall,
Three pink piglets up on the wall.

Three pink piglets up on the wall,
Three pink piglets,

If one of those piglets should happen to fall,
Two pink piglets up on the wall.

Two pink piglets up on the wall,
Two pink piglets,

If one of those piglets should happen to fall,
One pink piglet up on the wall.

One pink piglet up on the wall,
One pink piglet,

If that one piglet should happen to fall,

No pink piglets up on the wall.